For Alan, with love

First published in Great Britain in January 2015 by Bloomsbury Publishing Plc
Published in the United States of America in May 2016 by Bloomsbury Children's Books
www.bloomsbury.com

Bloomsbury is a registered trademark of Bloomsbury Publishing Plc

For information about permission to reproduce selections from this book, write to
Permissions, Bloomsbury Children's Books, 1385 Broadway, New York, New York 10018
Bloomsbury books may be purchased for business or promotional use. For information
on bulk purchases please contact Macmillan Corporate and Premium Sales Department at
specialmarkets@macmillan.com

Library of Congress Cataloging-in-Publication Data
available upon request
ISBN 978-1-68119-220-8 (hardcover)

Art created with mixed media
Typeset in Mr Lucky
Book design by Zoe Waring

Printed in China by Leo Paper Products, Heshan, Guangdong
1 3 5 7 9 10 8 6 4 2

All papers used by Bloomsbury Publishing, Inc., are natural, recyclable products
made from wood grown in well-managed forests. The manufacturing processes
conform to the environmental regulations of the country of origin.

WANTED!

Ralfy Rabbit, Book Burglar

Emily MacKenzie

BLOOMSBURY

NEW YORK LONDON OXFORD NEW DELHI SYDNEY

Some rabbits dreamed
of lettuce and carrots.

Others dreamed of flowering
meadows and juicy dandelions.

But Ralfy
was a
little bit
different...

Ralfy dreamed about **books.**
In fact, he didn't just dream about them . . .
he wanted to read **all** the time.

BUN FEST

Great food
Live music
Bunny Dance-Off

Ralfy's Reads

Alice in Warren Land

The Bunny with the
Radish Earring

The Catcher in the
Vegetable Patch

Around the Field
in 80 Days

ATTACK OF THE GIANT
FOX MONSTERS

My Favorites

THE HOPPIT

The Wind in
the Burrows

The Adventures
of Hucklebunny
Finn

The Magic Space
Dragon from Mars

The Secret
Vegetable Garden

The Moonlit
Vegetable Robbery

The Remains
of the Lettuce

Warren Peas

Books I must read soon

Muddy Mysteries

The 39 Lettuces

Foxy Favorites

The Rabbit with the Dandelion Tattoo

Drama and Dragons

A Hutch with a View

Wild Adventures

The Railway Rabbits

Bunniver's Travels

Books to tell Mom about

Wuthering Carrots

A Tale of Two Warrens

Books Dad might like

Gone with the Carrots

THE GOOD, THE BAD, AND THE BUNNY

One Flew over the Rabbit Hutch

Books to tell Tom and Betty about

The Rabbit, the Fox, and the Wardrobe

The Waterbunnies

He made lists of all the books he had read (and gave them carrot ratings).
He made lists of all the books he **wanted** to read
(and placed them in category order).
He even made lists of books to recommend to his family and friends.

Monkey EEEEEK! ME HEARTIES! YIKES! LANDLUBBER RAINFORES

OOOH AAAAH

Ralfy **loved** to learn new words.
He **loved** the smell of books
and the sound of the pages flipping.

He **loved** getting lost in stories, pretending he was the
captain of a pirate ship or an intrepid jungle explorer!

AHOY THERE

Swashbuckling CANOPY STRIPES

Pieces of eight

FOLIAGE PARROT Tige

JOLLY RO PROWL

AHOY SQUAWK!

I ♥ BOOKS

Yes, Ralfy **LOVED** books . . .

so much that he started **sneaking** into people's bedrooms
and reading their books while they were **sleeping!**

And then one thing led to another.

Ralfy didn't just **read** the books, he **took** them home!

He crept off with comics and cookbooks,
dashed away with dictionaries,
nabbed novels, and pinched poetry.

Ralfy had more books to read than ever before,
and he was very pleased with himself.

Arthur **loved** reading too.
He had shelves buckling with fairy tales, and bookcases
bursting with picture books. So when gaps started to appear
(along with half-eaten carrots and soggy lettuce leaves)
and his favorite book,
THE BIGGEST BOOK OF MONSTERS EVER,
went missing, Arthur noticed.

It was time to find out **WHO!**

Arthur assembled his special surveillance kit.
Then, with Teddy to keep him company,
he sat in the dark and waited . . . and waited.

A super Flashy Flashlight

BOOKS ON STRING

SNAPPY CAMERA

Teddy

Snacks
CHOCOWOCKO

Notebook and pencils

Binoculars

Chalk

STICKY TAPE

Soon he heard a rustle. Arthur frantically rummaged for his camera and his binoculars. He shined his flashlight into the dark corners of his room—and that's when he spotted Ralfy!

"STOP!

Come back here, you little bunny book thief,"

Arthur cried.

But it was too late!

Arthur was furious!

He told his mom, but she just laughed.
"A bunny book thief?
Arthur, I think your imagination is running wild."

He told his teacher, but
she just said, "Arthur, I want you to
go away and have a long, hard think about
what you are saying."

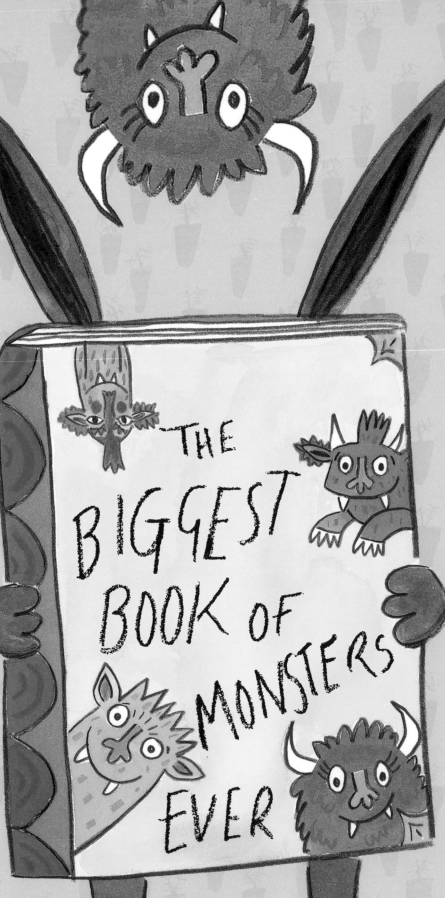

What could Arthur do?

That rascally rabbit had taken his favorite book of all time and **no one** believed him!

There was only one thing to do . . .

HELLO, HELLO, HELLO!

Arthur called his local police station.

"A bunny book thief, you say. Well, imagine that! Was there, ahem, anything unusual about this rabbit? Can you give me a description?" said Officer Puddle, snickering.

POLICE STATION HOTLINE

HA HA!

Meanwhile, Ralfy had found another
house with plenty of books to steal . . .

But this time Ralfy was in BIG trouble.

CAUGHT
IN THE ACT

BY A. POLICEMAN

He had burrowed up into Officer Puddle's house!
"Well, well, well, what have we here?" said Officer Puddle.
"Could it be a little bunny book thief? Arthur was right all along!"

Officer Puddle called Arthur right away and told him he had caught the culprit *read*-handed! "Please come to the police station first thing tomorrow to identify your bunny book thief!" he said.

Easy! thought Arthur. There can't be many rabbits who wear **I LOVE BOOKS** T-shirts!

But he was **wrong**. Arthur had never seen **so** many rabbits—
and they were all wearing them!
This was going to be harder than he thought.

But then, Officer Puddle pressed a big red button. An alarm bell rang and . . .

a conveyor belt of **goodies** started moving in front of the bunny lineup. As lettuce leaves, carrots, apples, and dandelions whizzed by, all the rabbits began to feast—except for **one**.

Ralfy just wasn't interested . . .

until a very **special** treat passed by . . .

Ralfy couldn't resist!
In a frenzy, he started flicking
through a pile of books.

"Aha! Gotcha!"
said Officer Puddle.
"You are in
BIG trouble!"

"I'm s-s-s-sorry!" stammered Ralfy.
"I just c-c-c-can't get enough books!"

"You can't just go
around **stealing** them,"
said Officer Puddle.
"You'll have to
put them all back!"

Suddenly Arthur began to feel sorry for Ralfy. After all, it was only because he loved books so much that he had managed to get himself into trouble. "If you want lots and lots of books to **borrow**," said Arthur, "I know **exactly** where you can get them . . ."

Ralfy and Arthur are best "book buddies" now
and love reading together whenever they can.
And they (especially Ralfy) **always** take the books back.

The library is their favorite place!

Note to reader: the next time you stop by your local library, be on the lookout—
you might, just might, spot Ralfy and Arthur reading there too!